Sheep Ahoy

Lee Kingman

Illustrated by Lisl Weil

Once there was a father, a Mr. Simpson, who was always saying "It's very simple!" Usually, whatever it was turned out to be not very simple at all, but his wife and children loved him and were always willing to help.

That's the way it went when Mr. Simpson decided to get rid of the cat-brier that grew all around the house. It was really very simple: just get some sheep to eat the cat-brier. When the sheep overrun the neighborhood, simple, just get a dog to tend the sheep; when the dog is afraid of the sheep, simple, just add a fence. But when sheep, dog, fence, house, and, of course, the cat-brier are threatened by fire, things get too simple for comfort.

The antics of this wonderfully wacky family, whose enthusiasm for the simple life leads to the merriest of complications, make a dozen laughs per page. And Lisl Weil's equally wacky illustrations never lose an opportunity to elaborate on the fun of Lee Kingman's story.

Sheep Ahoy

With pictures by LISL WEIL

Sheep Ahoy

by LEE KINGMAN

1 9 6 3

Houghton Mifflin Company Boston

The Riverside Press Cambridge

FOR
George,
Frank,
Ralph,
Michael,
Angela,
Millie,
Marie,
Julia,
and
Genevieve Bosson

ONCE there was a father, a Mr. Simpson, who was always saying, "It's very simple."

Usually whatever it was turned out not to be simple at all. But his family loved him very much. When things became difficult, they were always willing to help. Especially Suzi.

Suzi was seven when Mr. Simpson decided they should live in a house by a pond in some beautiful woods.

"It's a wonderful place where you can walk in the deep woods, and I love trees," said Mr. Simpson. So he moved Suzi and her mother and her four older brothers into the house.

It was very simple, really. Mrs. Simpson took

care of all the packing and unpacking. She found the cat when it ran away. She arranged the furniture and saw that the children were settled in their new schools.

"Nothing to it," said Mr. Simpson. "Now, who is coming out with me for a walk in our beautiful deep woods?"

"Not me," said Mrs. Simpson, falling into a deep chair and staying there.

"Not me," said Ralph, who was making a pirate ship to sail on the pond.

"Not me," said Michael, who was drawing plans for a control tower in the top of a maple tree.

"Not me," said George, who was building a model dinosaur.

"Not me," said Frank, who was reading a book.

"I'll go," said Suzi.

Two hours later, scratched, torn, and bleeding, Suzi and Mr. Simpson stumbled back from their walk in the beautiful deep woods.

"What has happened?" cried Mrs. Simpson.

"Are there tigers in the woods?" asked Frank.

"Or old Bronto-saur-us-es?" asked George.

"Or pirates?" hoped Ralph.

"There are wildcats!" teased Suzi.

"There are wild cat-briers," explained Mr. Simpson. "They are thorny plants that run wild. They even climb the trees and choke them."

"Isn't that sad!" sighed Mrs. Simpson.

"It's not that bad," said Mr. Simpson cheerfully. "We will put a fence around the woods. We will put sheep in the fence. And the sheep will eat all the cat-briers. I met a man who told me so. You see, it's all very simple."

Mr. Simpson was so enthusiastic that everyone wanted to help at once. Michael drew plans for a sheep shed. Ralph promised to build it. Frank brought books from the library and read all about sheep. George decided to be a veterinarian when he grew up.

"I shall learn to knit," declared Mrs. Simpson, "so we can use the wool."

With everyone so busy, of course it was Suzi and Mr. Simpson who dug the holes for the fence-posts. Then they stapled the fence into place. Finally a truck arrived with five fat ewes and one fine ram.

"Those are Hampshires," explained Frank.

"Healthy-looking sheep," agreed George.

"They'll make lovely sweaters," said Mrs. Simpson.

"How are we going to get them inside the fence?" asked Suzi. "We forgot to put in a gate!"

"It's very simple!" cried Mr. Simpson. "I'll lift them over and that will be that."

Suzi named each one as Mr. Simpson heaved it over the fence. "There goes Sarah. Stella. Sally. Selma. Sue. And, of course, Sam."

Strong Mr. Simpson was tired after lifting the sheep. And no sooner had he put Sam down inside

the fence than the ram
backed up and high-jumped
right over the fence and out.
"Isn't he wonderful!" shouted Suzi.

"How are you going to catch him?" cried Mrs. Simpson.

Sam jumped and sprang as if each of his legs was a Pogo stick.

"It's very simple, really," said Mr. Simpson. "Boys, while I open up the fence here for a gate, you hop on your bicycles. Round up the ram!"

The boys hopped on their bikes and rode round and around. Mr. Simpson and Suzi fixed a gate as quickly as they could. Luckily Sam was so dizzy from the bicycle rodeo that he was glad to be led through the gate.

For a few weeks everything was fine. The sheep

wandered about making tunnels in the cat-brier, eating whatever grass and weeds they could find.

Suzi sat on a fencepost for hours, talking to them and scratching their heads. George took notes on their health and habits. Michael sketched them. (Sam moved so quickly that Michael usually drew him with eight legs.) Ralph built the sheep shed. Frank read all the stories he could find about sheep, right back to the tale of Jason and the Golden Fleece.

But the sheep grew tired of munching briers.

Outside the fence was a glorious green world. One by one the sheep jumped the fence. They began eating their way across the lawn.

On the green grass by the pond, the boys were playing badminton. Suzi was keeping score.

"The sheep are out!" Suzi suddenly yelled.

Waving their badminton rackets, the boys hopped on their bikes. They briskly rounded up the sheep while Suzi opened the gate.

This happened every morning for a week. Finally Mrs. Simpson suggested something should be done.

"We shall put bells on them," decided Mr. Simpson. "Then *if* they should *ever* get out again, we will hear them right away. We can chase them back before they do any damage. It's quite simple, you see."

Mr. Simpson bought a string of Indian temple bells. He and Suzi tied a bell on each sheep. They listened in delight as the sheep shook their heads. The bells rang out, all different tones, in a tangle of music.

"Could we teach them to play a tune?" asked Suzi.

"It would be fun. But I don't have time just now," said her father.

"That's all right," said Suzi. "We can listen to it wild."

The sound was lovely, singing down from the woods in the twilight.

Then suddenly there was a jangle of bells outside the front door.

"The sheep are out!" called Mrs. Simpson.

The boys grabbed up their badminton rackets and dashed out. The next thing Mr. Simpson knew, he heard a man yelling, "Help! Help! Call off your boys!"

Mr. and Mrs. Simpson and Suzi rushed out. There was an angry Ice-Cream man.

"I'm so sorry!" cried Mr. Simpson. "We thought your bell — was our sheep. Well, we'll have two ice creams each for everybody."

The Ice-Cream man drove away and never came back, which saved the Simpsons a lot of money. Until Suzi bought so much bread from the Bakery Truck man.

"It's the only way I can get the sheep back in the fence by myself," she explained. "I show them some bread. Then I run up and throw it inside the fence. And they jump in after it."

"That's using your head!" said Mr. Simpson proudly.

"But the bread bills are terrible," moaned Mrs. Simpson. "There must be another way of putting the sheep back where they belong."

"There is!" exclaimed Mr. Simpson. "Why didn't I think of it before. It's so simple. We'll get a sheep dog to take care of the sheep."

Finally Mr. Simpson and Suzi found a farm

where there were five fuzzy black-and-white
puppies.

"Someone told me they were Border Collies,"
said the farmer. "But you have to train them, you
know."

"Oh, that's simple," said Mr. Simpson. "Any-
body can teach a dog tricks."

"You don't say!" said the farmer. "Which one
do you want?"

"That one." Suzi pointed
to the friendliest
and fuzziest.

"You sure?" asked
the farmer.

"He's the prettiest,"
said Suzi, hugging
the puppy.

"It's your choice," said the farmer. He took Mr. Simpson's money, and added, after he waved them away in the car, "He's the friendliest and the fuzziest and the prettiest. But he's not the smartest."

Suzi carried the puppy to meet the sheep. She put him down by the fence. "Here is Sheppy," she announced. For what other name could a sheep dog have? "He will take care of you."

The biggest ewe, Sarah, stamped her foot and burped, "Baa-aa!" at him.

Sam lowered his head and butted the nearest fencepost till it shivered.

Sheppy scampered away, howling for his mother and all the comforts of the old farm.

Suzi scolded the sheep. "You shouldn't frighten the dog who's going to take care of you!" She

took Sheppy in the house and tucked him into her
doll's cradle for a nap.

Sheppy loved the cradle. He loved Suzi and
the boys. He didn't like the sheep at all.

When autumn came, Mr. Simpson bought big

bales of hay and stacked them in the shed. The sheep no longer jumped the fence. They stood around and chewed hay all day instead.

"My!" exclaimed Mrs. Simpson. "We're saving money now on ice cream and bread. But the bills for dog food and hay are terrible."

"Don't fret," explained Mr. Simpson. "When we shear the sheep in the spring, think of all the money you'll save knitting sweaters. And next fall, we'll have two or three sheep to eat, so we'll save on meat."

"Never!" cried Mrs. Simpson, George, Frank, Ralph, Michael, and Suzi. "Never will we eat any lamb, mutton, or chops while we have sheep."

"That's good!" said Mr. Simpson with a tremendous sigh of relief. "I couldn't eat any lamb, mutton, or chops, either."

All through the winter the sheep grew bigger and fatter. Sheppy grew longer and lazier. In

March on a crisp snowy morning, Mr. Simpson rushed in from the shed crying, "Lambs! Lambs! Spring is here! Sarah has twins!"

Everyone hurried out to wonder at the wobbly twins. Next morning Stella had a lamb, and then Sally had twins, and soon Selma and Sue also had lambs.

When she wasn't asleep or in school, Suzi stayed out in the sheep shed. One morning she found Sarah's twins looked thin and weak. Sarah was sick.

Mr. Simpson called the vet. Dr. Shepherd came and said, "You'll have to bottle-feed those twins. And bring that ewe over to my office every afternoon for a week for treatment."

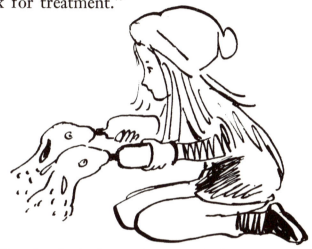

Suzi loved feeding lambs before school and after school. But no one, not even the boys who usually begged to stay up late, enjoyed feeding them in the cold sheep shed at midnight.

"The simplest thing to do," decided Mr. Simpson, "is bring them in the house for a while."

So he tucked a lamb under each arm and took them in the house.

"Oh, dear!" said Mrs. Simpson. "Well, put them in a box in the kitchen."

The next morning the lambs stood up and baa-ed so loudly for food that they woke every one up. When they were stronger, the lambs found they could jump out of the box. They ran and leaped and tripped and slid on their noses. They skidded over the shiny floors and hid under tables and chairs. Sheppy was so hurt by all the attention paid to them that he slunk into a corner to sulk.

"I just love lambs," sighed Mrs. Simpson. "Outdoors."

"Once you start bottle-feeding them, you have to keep on for three months," explained Suzi. "And you can't put them out now they're used to a warm house. But I have an idea!"

Suzi set her old playpen up in the living room.

The lambs stood inside, crying "Baa-aa" in their squeaky voices, and tried to get out. But they couldn't. Suzi brought all her friends home from school to see them.

She also helped Mr. Simpson take Sarah over to Dr. Shepherd. It was hard lifting Sarah into the car. But the big ewe soon enjoyed the rides.

She liked to sit on the back seat and look out the
window. So Suzi sat beside her and pointed things
out to her. The last day they went, Suzi took one
of her mother's Easter hats and tied it on Sarah's
head. They stopped traffic on Main Street.
A newsman took a picture
that was printed in the

paper. Mrs. Simpson never wore that hat again.

At the end of the first year, Mr. Simpson was pleased with his flock of five fat ewes, one fine ram, and eight lambs. When the cat-brier began poking out its first tender leaves in May, he was delighted to see the sheep eating them.

"You see!" he said triumphantly. "Getting rid of cat-brier is very simple. Just keep sheep."

But in June Mr. Simpson had to take a vacation from his job at the office because there were so many things to do for the sheep. "Some day," he hoped loudly, "I'll have a job where I can work at home. It would make keeping sheep very simple indeed."

First he had to learn how to shear the sheep with electric clippers. It was hot, heavy work.

"Look how skinny the sheep really are!" Suzi

was surprised to see how small they were with their wool off.

So were the sheep. They hid in the bushes, quite ashamed of themselves.

Mrs. Simpson sent off two big bags of wool. When a large box of yarn came back, she knit and she knit.

Finally she said to Suzi, "You will just have to learn to knit, too, or we'll never use up all this yarn."

So Suzi did. She knit extra-long scarves and small nose-warmers for each of her brothers.

Then there was hay to make in a field beyond the pond. Mr. Simpson used a scythe and Suzi used a sickle. The boys raked the hay and turned it. When it was dry, they piled it into four big haymows. Then what a grand time they had sliding on the haymows and hiding in them!

Everyone was busy because of the sheep. Except Sheppy. He lay lazily around.

"You are some sheep dog!" Mr. Simpson told him. "Don't you know you ought to be busy doing something?"

"The farmer said we'd have to train him," Suzi

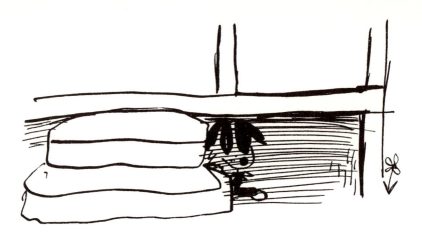

remembered. So she spent hours teaching him to "sit" and "lie down."

But whenever the sheep broke out, Sheppy hid under the porch.

Mr. Simpson was puzzled. "Maybe he isn't old enough to train yet."

"I know what's the matter!" cried Suzi. "The sheep scared him that very first day. Maybe if we let him play with one of the lambs, he'd make friends. Then he won't be afraid of the sheep any more."

"We could try," said Mr. Simpson. "It just might be as simple as that."

He carried one of Sarah's twins into the yard. Suzi put Sheppy on his leash. But as soon as Sheppy saw the lamb, he lay down and shut his eyes. Suzi let go of his leash in disgust.

Then the lamb decided to be friendly. She bounced over and began sniffing the dog. Sheppy jumped up and ran toward the pond. The lamb thought he wanted to play and chased after him.

"Look out!" yelled Mr. Simpson. Suzi skipped out of the way just as big Sarah went thundering across the lawn looking for her lamb. The next thing they knew, all three animals were floundering in the pond.

Luckily, Ralph and Michael were sailing on their pirate craft. "We'll rescue the lamb!" they called, splashing toward it.

Sheppy swam to the far side and dashed ashore. But poor Sarah swam in frantic circles, baa-ing angrily for her lamb.

Mr. Simpson hopped into his tiny boat. He rowed as fast as he could. Somehow he hauled

the tired sheep into the boat. Sarah sat there drip-
ping and cross. The boat sank lower and lower
in the water. Mr. Simpson barely made it back to
shore!

Sarah shook herself so hard that Mr. Simpson
looked as if he'd taken a shower.

Sheppy waited until the sheep were back inside
the fence before he dared come home.

"How can he ever learn what to do, if he won't even try to get along with the sheep?" Even Suzi was upset with Sheppy.

"We'll just have to be extra careful not to let the sheep out of the fence for any reason whatsoever."

But as the leaves on the briers grew tough and dry in the summer heat, the grass and the flowers in the Simpsons' yard looked more beautiful than ever. Mrs. Simpson was proud of her flowers. So she invited some friends to afternoon tea in the garden.

The ladies were sitting peacefully with their tea and cookies when the sheep burst out of the fence.

The big ones sailed over. The little ones wiggled under. They raced for the flowers.

Before Mrs. Simpson could do anything but screech, Sarah ate the calendulas, Stella ate the carnations, Sally ate the bachelor's buttons, Selma ate the African daisies, Sue ate the Sweet Williams and Sam ate the snapdragons. The lambs ate the petunias. Then they all headed for the tea party.

The ladies jumped up shrieking, as Sam tipped over the tea cart.

"Shoo!" cried Mrs. Simpson. "Shoo! Shoo! Shoo! Where are the boys! Where is Mr. Simpson! Where is Suzi! Where is that useless Sheppy!"

Mr. Simpson and the boys and Sheppy were as far away from a ladies' tea party as they could go — way up in the woods. But Suzi, who was hiding

overhead in an apple tree, came swinging down. She grabbed a plate of cookies.

"Bread!" she shouted to the sheep. Then she ran to the fence and threw the cookies in. The sheep jumped in and ate them all up. Suzi counted the sheep. They were all in, safe and sound.

But Mrs. Simpson was unhappy. She was even more unhappy the next morning when she found the sheep had jumped the fence again in the night. They ate up all the flowers they missed at the party. Then they went to sleep under the garden chairs, all except Sarah's twins, who were curled up together on the chaise longue.

"Somebody must do something about those sheep!" shouted Mrs. Simpson, staring at Mr. Simpson. "Or I am going to get rid of them."

"Now, Mother," said Mr. Simpson, which only made Mrs. Simpson madder. "How can I get rid of the cat-brier without the sheep?"

"Please don't get rid of the sheep!" cried George, Frank, Ralph, and Michael. "Think of all the work we did for them — building the fence —"

"Huh!" said Suzi and Mr. Simpson.

"Well, the shed anyway. And making all that hay! Who is going to eat the hay if the sheep don't?"

"We'll have a year's worth of Shredded Hay for breakfast," said Mrs. Simpson crossly.

"Think of how disappointed Sheppy will be when he discovers he's a sheep dog — and he doesn't have any sheep!" Suzi reminded her mother.

"I am thinking!" said Mrs. Simpson grimly. But when she saw all the unhappy faces staring at her, she said, "All right. I'll give the sheep one more chance. But next time they jump that fence — away they go!"

Suzi whistled to Sheppy. She made him sit. "Sheppy, this is serious. You are our only chance. You've got to stop just dogging around. You must learn how to herd those sheep. But how am I going to teach you?"

She thought for a while. Then she called the boys to help her. "Remember the white sweaters Mother knit you — that are too big? And the nose-warmers? If you put those on, and you use the scarves for tails, and you get down on your hands and knees and you baa, maybe I can show Sheppy how to herd you."

Frank remembered what he'd read about training sheep dogs, so he told Suzi what to do. Every day the boys put their knitted things on and crawled around, baa-ing. But they usually ended up in a wild wrestling match with Sheppy. He

enjoyed it so much he came running to meet them after school, carrying a long white scarf in his mouth so they wouldn't forget his training.

"See?" Suzi said hopefully. "He really is smart."

"Let's hope so," worried Mr. Simpson. "We'd all miss the sheep terribly if Mother sent them away."

But Suzi didn't tell her father the only result of

the training so far. Sheppy now liked to sit outside the fence and bark joyfully at the sheep — just
the way he barked at the woolly boys.   The sheep
liked to shake their heads, stamp their feet, and
burp "Baa-aa" back at him.

"At least they are all speaking to each other
now," said Suzi.

Then one fine October afternoon, Mrs. Simpson took Sheppy for a long walk in the woods. Suddenly she smelled smoke. She looked up and saw scarves of smoke flung over the tops of the trees.

"There's a forest fire! Sheppy, which is the quickest way home?"

The wind was brisk and the woods were dry. Flames crackled up from the bushes and jumped from tree to tree.

Sheppy couldn't smell the right way to run home and Mrs. Simpson was confused in the swirl of smoke.

Then Sheppy sat down in the path, threw back his head and howled. He listened and howled again.

Faintly through the woods came the answering "Baa-aa" of the sheep. Sheppy trotted toward the

sound and Mrs. Simpson trotted after. The fire crackled after them. Whenever they stopped, lost, Sheppy barked. The sheep baa-ed. Soon Mrs.

Simpson could hear their bells. What a lovely sound it was!

Mrs. Simpson had never been so glad to see all the sheep as she was when she came rushing out of the woods, with the flames licking along behind her.

"Jump!" she yelled to the sheep. "Chase 'em!" she yelled to Sheppy as she scrambled over the fence.

The sheep followed her over, big ones high-jumping, little ones wiggling under. Except Sam. He and Sheppy stood barking and baa-ing at each other.

Mrs. Simpson whistled. Sheppy ran for the fence — but it seemed too high for him. And he was too big to wiggle through like a lamb.

"Oh, dear!" Mrs. Simpson tried to open the

gate and everything stuck. "Oh, dear! Sam, chase Sheppy!"

Sam didn't have to be told. He was going to do it anyway. He stamped his feet, rumbled a most ferocious "Baaa" and charged Sheppy.

Sheppy was so scared he jumped right over the

high fence with no trouble at all, with Sam right behind him.

Mrs. Simpson and the sheep and the dog all ran

toward the house. A fire engine came clanging into the yard and snorted to a stop.

"Spotted your smoke from the fire tower!" called a fireman. "Looks like a big one!"

He radioed for more help.

Soon four more engines and hundreds of feet of hose tangled the yard. A pumping engine chugged by the pond. People poured out of cars and lugged heavy fire cans full of water into the woods. Even Dr. Shepherd, driving home from a call on a sick cow, stopped to help.

Suzi and the boys biked home from school. Lots of friends came with them. The boys grabbed Mrs. Simpson's pots and pans out of the kitchen and ran about pouring water on sparks and hot spots at the edge of the woods.

The girls wanted to help, too. So they found

trays and glasses and carried drinks of water around to the brave boys fighting the fire.

Mrs. Simpson ran indoors to save some things

in case the house burned down. She wrapped them up and carried them out. But when she saw all the people in the yard that she had never seen before in her life, she carried the things back in the house again.

She spent the rest of the fire counting George, Frank, Ralph, Michael and Suzi whenever they dashed by.

When Mr. Simpson finally drove into the yard after his hard day at the office, he was flabbergasted to find the fire engines and all the people.

"Where are my wife and children!" he shouted.

"Here!" called Mrs. Simpson.

"Here!" called Suzi and the boys.

"And where are my sheep and my sheep dog?"

"I'm looking for your sheep, too," said Dr. Shepherd, putting down a fire can. "Did you say you had a sheep dog? He's probably taking good care of them then."

"Huh!" snorted the boys.

"He's a Border Collie. But he's a little shy. With the sheep," Suzi explained. "There they are!"

She pointed to the lawn by the pond. There was Sheppy, surrounded by sheep. He sat trembling in their midst, while they stared down their long noses at him.

"There's my sheep dog!" said Mr. Simpson proudly.

"Your *what* dog?" asked Dr. Shepherd. He

looked closely at Sheppy and chuckled. "I'm afraid he's not a real Border Collie. He does look a great deal like one. But he's a little too big and his head is too wide. He's bordering on a Border Collie — but that's all."

"No wonder he didn't have any built-in sheep sense," sighed Mr. Simpson.

"Never mind, Sheppy!" Suzi threw her arms around his neck. "You don't have to be a sheep dog any more. You can be a people dog and take care of us instead."

You never saw a happier dog!

But when Mr. Simpson came back from a walk through his sad black woods, he was miserable.

"At least the cat-brier is gone. Maybe the simplest thing would have been to burn it out in the beginning. But my fenceposts are all gone, too. We'll never be able to keep the sheep out of the gardens now. We'll just have to get rid of them. Oh, dear! I am so fond of the stupid things."

"So are we!" cried Suzi and the boys.

"So am I!" Mrs. Simpson surprised them all. "They saved my life! And Sheppy's, too. If they hadn't baa-ed for us and rung their bells, and chased us over the fence, we wouldn't be here now."

"What can we do?"

They stared at each other, thinking and thinking. Mr. Simpson stared at the sheep by the pond.

"I have it!" he cried. "It's the simplest thing in the world! Of course it will take a little work — and a little time — and a little money."

He wouldn't tell them what it was. For a week he drew plans and phoned all kinds of people. Then Mr. Simpson paced off a large circle around

the house and the gardens. A crew came with bull-dozers. When Mrs. Simpson began to worry about her spring bulbs, Mr. Simpson sent her and the children away for a week.

When they came back and saw Mr. Simpson's simple solution, they couldn't have been happier. What a wonderful man he was to think of it!

"See!" he exclaimed, waving his hand. "The sheep are out — but we're in!"

I'm happy to tell you that the Simpsons for a whole year now have had all the fun of a moat around their house and gardens. It's deep enough and wide enough so the sheep won't swim across it. But the sheep can see the lovely flowers and the green grass, just teasingly beyond them across the moat. So they stay hopefully in sight of it. They wouldn't think of wandering away.

Sheppy has turned out to be a fine watchdog.
He lies in a special doghouse, built like a sentry
box, and guards the drawbridge. When any one

comes to the bridge, Sheppy barks until the
Simpsons decide whether or not they will let down
the drawbridge.

Mrs. Simpson recommends a moat as the best way to save money on everything from ice cream to encyclopedias. Suzi and the boys give wonderful parties with swimming and diving and canoeing in summer. And skating in winter.

And Mr. Simpson now has his heart's desire. He has left his office job and works at home where he can enjoy the simple pleasures of being a shepherd and a businessman and a father all at the same time.

He's very busy designing Simpson's Simple Home Protectors for people all over the country who like to have the very newest thing — moats, of course.